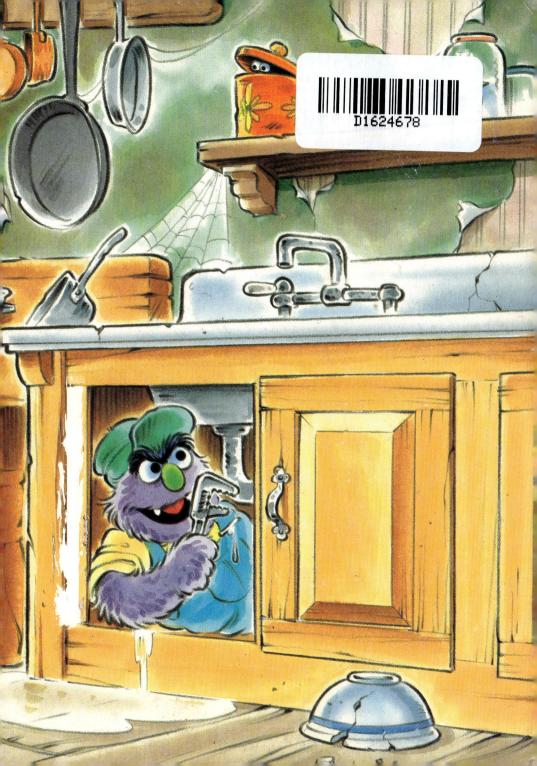

Monster in the parlor?

Monster in the bathroom?

Monster in the bedroom?

Monsters in the garden?

Monster in the window?

Monster in the hallway?

Monster in the nursery?

Are there monsters in the basement?

In the attic, too?

Monsters all around the house
want to PLAY with you.